As Time
Went By

I would like to thank my father, José, my mother, Cecilia,
and my brothers, Alberto and Edgar,
passengers on the first ship I ever drew.

First published in the United States and Canada in 2016 by NorthSouth Books, Inc.,
an imprint of NordSüd Verlag AG, CH-8005 Zürich, Switzerland.

Distributed in the United States by NorthSouth Books, Inc., New York 10016.
Library of Congress Cataloging-in-Publication Data is available.

ISBN: 978-0-7358-4248-9
Printed in Lithuania by BALTO print, Vilnius, October 2015
1 3 5 7 9 · 10 8 6 4 2

www.northsouth.com

José Sanabria

As Time Went By

North
South

Part One

Once upon a time there was a ship
that sailed beside the sun
with very important people on board.

As time went by, the ship was sold
to a merchant.

And then to a fishing company.

As time went by,
the ship was abandoned.

Completely abandoned...

Part Two

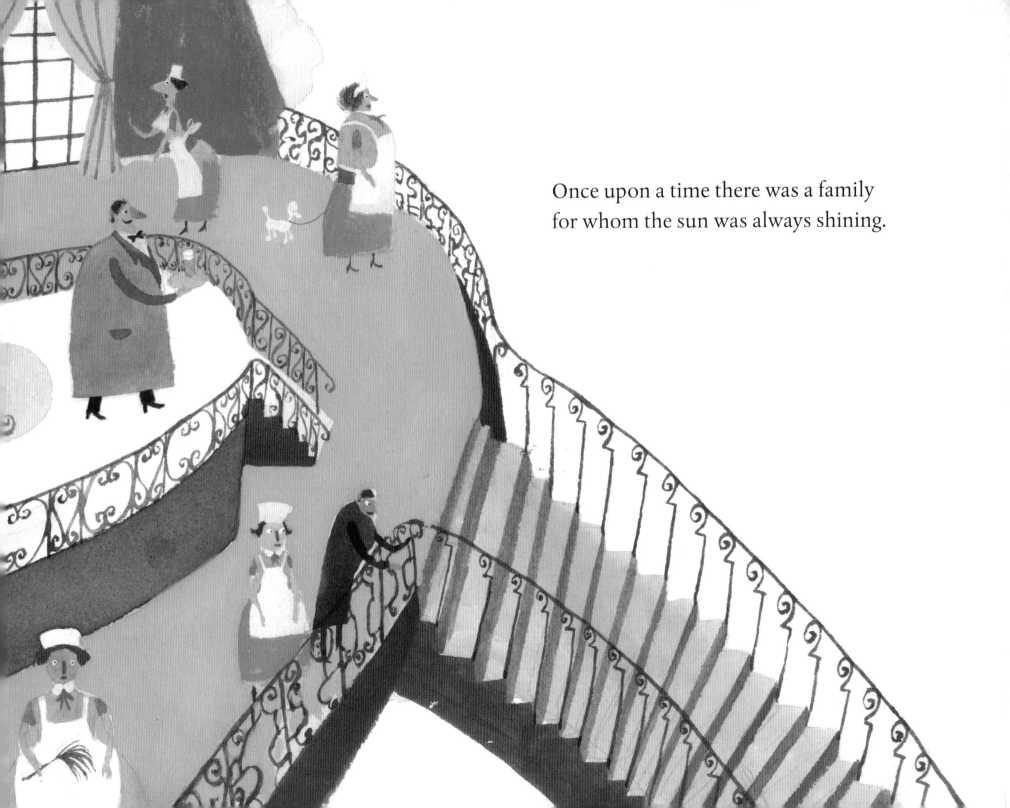

Once upon a time there was a family
for whom the sun was always shining.

As time went by, luxury and excess made the family poor, and they had to move to a small house.

And then to an even smaller house.

As time went by, the family lost what little it had left
and had no choice but to live in a village near the harbor
alongside other people who had also lost everything.

One morning a man came and said that he owned
the village land and pushed the residents out.
They all had to go to a place where the sun was gray
and did not shine.

Part Three

Once upon a time there was a village of
homeless people and an abandoned ship.

As time went by, the people rebuilt the ship
with the help of a man who had loved the sea
since he was a boy and knew a lot.

Working together, man and villagers,
they fixed the ship so it could sail again.

As time went by, the people loved and took care
of the ship since it was their new home.

Once upon a time there was a ship
that sailed beside the sun
with very important people on board.

José Sanabria is a Colombian illustrator based in Argentina since 1992.
He studied graphic design in Bogotá and illustration in Buenos Aires.
His teachers were Juan Bobillo, Marcelo Sosa, and Oscar Rojas.
His works have been exhibited at the Biennale of Bratislava, at the Bologna
Children's Book Fair, and in other collective exhibitions in Argentina,
Italy, Germany, and Poland. He has published about fifteen books in
Colombia, Argentina, Spain, France, and Germany.